Snowville

To Jordyn
Keep believing

Snowville

By

Brian A. Webster

Illustrated by

Stephanie L. Wilkins

Plymouth, MI, U.S.A.
www.PublishHMSI.com

Snowville

Published by HMSI Publishing L.L.C., a division of HMSI, inc.
www.PublishHMSI.com

By
Brian A. Webster

Illustrations and Cover Layout by
Stephanie L. Wilkins

Edited by
Monica Tombers and Stephanie L. Wilkins

Publishing Coordination by
Jessica A. Paredes

Published by
David R. Haslam

For information about permissions to reproduce any part of this work, write to

Permissions,
HMSI Publishing L.L.C.
50768 Van Buren Drive,
Plymouth, MI 48170, U.S.A.

info@PublishHMSI.com
Tel: 1.734.259.0387

ISBN – 13: 978-0-9826945-5-8
Library of Congress: 2010940054

0069-0001
TKR 10 9 8 7 6 5 4 3 2 1
MK 31527-23898
40476 23:25

Printed in the United States of America

To the REAL Hailey

Never let your dreams melt away.

Hailey watches as her older brother Ryan plops a worn black hat on top of a snowman's head. She reaches down, scoops up a mound of snow and adds it to the snowman's belly. "I can hardly wait for tomorrow. I wonder what Santa will bring me," she says as she pats the snow into place.

"You really think a fat guy from the North Pole flies around the world delivering presents?" Ryan snickers. "Sorry, but reindeer can't fly and there's no such thing as Santa Claus."

"Yes there is! I'm telling Mom what you said," blurts Hailey as she brushes a tear from her face.

Just then, their mom leans her head out the front door and calls, “Time for dinner!”

Ryan dashes into the house leaving Hailey alone with the snowman. She sighs and gazes into its coal eyes. “He’s wrong, you know,” she says to the snowman, but it just stares back. Sadly, she turns away and trudges toward the house as darkness settles over the yard.

Unable to sleep, Hailey stares out her window as huge flakes fall from the dark sky. Suddenly, a truck pulls up across the street and she sounds out the letters written on the side: North Pole Ice Company. “I’ll show him there is a Santa Claus,” she whispers. She runs to her closet and quickly pulls on her warmest clothes.

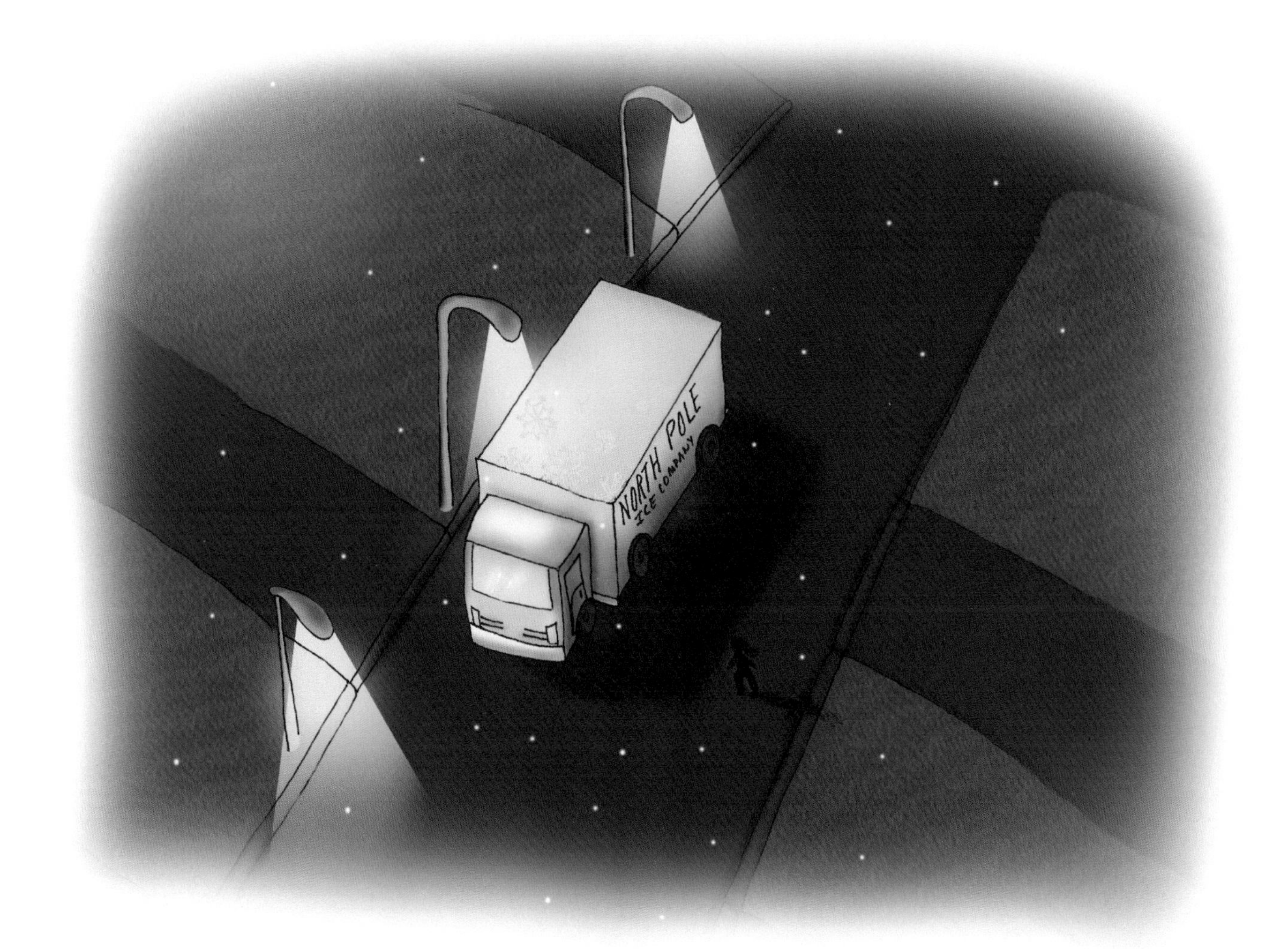

Quietly Hailey opens the window and climbs out into the crisp night air. Dangling her feet over the sill, she jumps to the ground and dashes to the other side of the street. She tries the handle on the driver's side of the truck. It's unlocked, so she pulls herself up and climbs inside. Behind the seat is a space just big enough for her to lie down. As she squeezes in she spots an old blanket and hides beneath it.

Hailey holds her breath when she hears the truck door open. The seat moves slightly as the driver settles into it. When the truck door slams shut and the engine starts Hailey relaxes and takes a deep breath. The hum of the motor and the truck motion soon lull Hailey to sleep. Hours later the truck comes to a stop. Hailey's eyes pop open. She hears the driver leave the cab. Quickly she climbs out the passenger door.

Hailey blinks in the bright sunlight. In the distance she sees sleds zipping down a steep hill next to a small town nestled in a valley. Hailey decides to investigate.

As she approaches the village, she discovers that everyone there is made of snow. Fascinated, she stares at the strange sight as snow people bustle from shop to shop. Hailey doesn't notice everyone staring at her as she curiously peeks into shop windows. Suddenly she begins to shiver, and she realizes that she's all alone and does not know where to go.

Hailey looks up at a banner stretching over Main Street. The words are too hard for her to read. She jumps when a voice comes from behind her. “Hi, my name’s Crystal. What’s your name?”

Hailey turns to see a snowgirl. “You can speak?” she asks.

“Of course. Why wouldn’t I?” Crystal replies with a smile.

Shyly, Hailey smiles back. “I’m Hailey.”

“May I call you Hail?” asks Crystal. “That’s a really cool name.”

Hailey nods and smiles.

“What does that sign say?” she asks, pointing up at the banner.

“Snowville Christmas Snow Festival,” Crystal says. “It’s tonight!”

Hailey suddenly remembers why she came to the North Pole. “Where can I find Santa?”

“Oh... you don’t want to go there! To get to Santa’s workshop you have to cross through the Black Ice Forest. Frigid Von Blizzard, the ice witch, lives there and she turns snowpeople into ice!”

"Let's go sledding," Crystal suggests, motioning to the snowchildren on the hill.

Hailey is freezing but she doesn't want to disappoint her new friend so she replies, "I'd love to." Over and over they zoom down the hill, laughing and screaming with excitement. Together, they pull the sled back up the hill.

Finally Crystal says, "It's getting late. I should go home."

"You aren't from around here, are you, Hail?" asks Crystal.

"Um, no, I rode here in an ice truck," says Hailey.

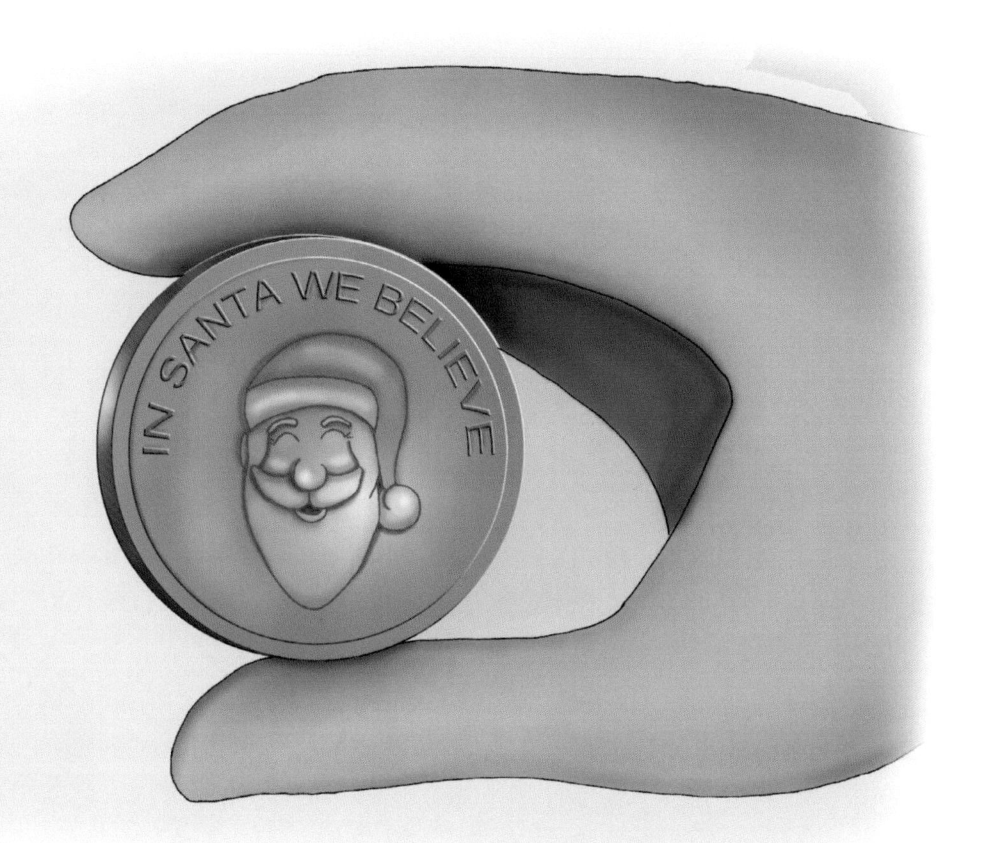

Crystal holds up a shiny silver coin. “I have a souvenir for you.” She hands Hailey a coin with a picture of Santa on it.

The reflection of the sun on the coin nearly blinds Hailey as she tries to read the inscription, “IN... SANTA...”

“WE BELIEVE,” Crystal finishes.

Hailey stares at it before remembering to say, “Thanks.” Pocketing the coin, she adds, “I really need to see Santa.”

“I told you, no one can go to Santa’s workshop. I’m afraid you came all this way for nothing,” says Crystal.

Hailey begins to cry. Concerned, Crystal asks, “What’s wrong?”

Hailey sniffles and wipes her eyes on her sleeve. “I don’t have anywhere to go and I don’t know how I will get home for Christmas.”

“You can come home with me! Maybe we can figure something out,” replies Crystal.

When they arrive at Crystal’s house, her family greets Hailey with a hug. Hailey’s sadness disappears as she, Crystal and Flake, Crystal’s brother, busily make snow cones for the evening festival.

As they work, Crystal explains, “The whole village will turn out for the Snow Festival. Each year the mayor of Snowville draws the name of one snowchild who may accompany Santa on his trip around the world. I have never been chosen. Wouldn’t it be fun if I won?”

Later when everyone is gathered at the festival, they wait for the mayor to draw a name and make the announcement. “This year the lucky winner is... Crystal!” Everyone cheers; Hailey loudest of all!

Suddenly a scream pierces through the crowd. Crystal's mom cries, "My baby is missing!" Flake is nowhere to be found.

The mayor calls for a search party. Tracks leading into the Black Ice Forest are found by the tree line, but no one wants to cross into Frigid Von Blizzard's territory.

Hailey wants to help her new friends find Flake, so she boldly shouts "I'll go."

"But the ice witch...," whispers Crystal.

Bravely Hailey steps into the Black Ice Forest. She darts between the trees, keeping an eye out for Frigid Von Blizzard. She passes many ice sculptures who were once snowpeople, but none of them are Flake. Finally she spots him, frozen solid.

Suddenly a dark, eerie shadow covers Hailey. She turns to find Frigid Von Blizzard glaring down at her. "You dare trespass on my territory?" the witch cackles as she beams her Icicle Wand toward Hailey. Hailey's eyes dart side to side. She is all alone.

As Hailey puts her shaking hands in her pockets, she feels the smooth Santa coin. Swiftly she holds it in front of her and whispers, "IN SANTA WE BELIEVE, IN SANTA WE BELIEVE!"

Frigid Von Blizzard blows a gust of frozen crystals toward Hailey. The shiny coin reflects the witch's icy crystals, sending them back at her.

Trapped by her own magic, Frigid Von Blizzard is instantly frozen. Her spell is broken and all of the snowpeople come back to life. Overjoyed, Hailey grabs Flake's hand and leads everyone out of the Black Ice Forest.

As they leave, the black ice changes into sparkling white crystals and the forest becomes a glistening snow haven.

The whole town is waiting as the snowpeople burst through the trees. A cheer erupts. There are plenty of hugs and tears as families reunite.

Crystal throws her arms around Hailey. “My hero!” she exclaims, and hands her the Santa Pass. “This belongs to you!”

“But I’m not a snowkid. What if Santa won’t let me go with him?” Hailey asks.

The mayor steps up onto a nearby stump. “Attention! Attention! For bravery and courage I proclaim Hailey an honorary citizen of Snowville!”

Crystal and the townspeople pack Hailey with snow, making her look like one of them. Hailey shivers, but her heart is warm. The townspeople lead Hailey to the top of the next hill. She looks down to see Santa's workshop. She turns, waves and then zips down the hill as fast as her snow covered legs will carry her.

Standing in front of huge doors, Hailey swipes her Santa Pass through the card reader. The doors swing open. As she enters the workshop she sees a frenzy of activity. Elves hustle from one workbench to another.

Mrs. Claus greets Hailey with a cup of cold chocolate, the favorite drink of Snowville. “You must be Hailey, this year’s winner,” she says, “Welcome, please wait here. I’ll let Santa know you’ve arrived.”

Across the room Hailey spots a fireplace with blazing logs. She crosses the room and stands with her back to the fire watching all the activity. The heat feels so good.

When Santa bursts into the workshop, Hailey jumps excitedly. Clumps of slushy snow fall from her backside. “Well, well” exclaims Santa. “You must be Hailey!”

“I-I-am,” stammers Hailey.

“Just so you know,” announces Santa, “as an honorary Snowville citizen, you do qualify for the Santa Pass.”

“I knew there was a Santa and now I can get home!” Hailey exclaims.

Before Hailey knows it, Santa's sleigh is packed, the team of reindeer is hitched and Santa is ready to leave. Mrs. Claus and the elves cheer as the sleigh carrying Hailey and Santa is lifted into the air.

The people of Snowville cheer and wave as they fly over the tiny village. Quick as a wink Santa begins stopping the sleigh at one house after another. Hailey watches in fascination as Santa zips down chimneys with presents.

Before she knows it Hailey spots her own house. She can see Mom calling Ryan and herself in to dinner. Everything looks just like it did the evening she left for the North Pole. Hailey turns to Santa with questioning eyes!

Santa winks and says, “You’ll be back before your family even misses you. I wouldn’t want you in any trouble because of me.”

Hailey reaches over to give Santa a hug and says, “This is the best Christmas I have ever had.”

A second later, Hailey magically finds herself standing next to the snowman she and Ryan made. As she watches Santa's sleigh disappear into the evening sky her mother comes down from the porch. "What are you looking at?"

"Why, Santa of course," Hailey says.

"Come in the house, it's freezing out there. You know you're not made of snow."

Ryan snickers at Hailey and starts to follow. Something shiny on the ground catches his eye. Picking it up, he studies the coin. Written on it is: IN SANTA WE BELIEVE. Puzzled, he glances up at the sky in time to see a small speck of light disappear over the horizon.

"Santa?" Ryan asks, turning to the snowman.

The snowman winks.

Acknowledgements

I'd like to thank David R. Haslam, my publisher, and his team for believing in Snowville. I also want to give thanks to Monica, for editing, Jessica, the coordinator, and Stephanie, for editing and bringing my vision to life through her illustrations.

Finally, my biggest heartfelt thanks go to my family, especially my wife Cathy for her support and my children who provide the inspiration for my stories.

About the Author

Brian A. Webster is a Detroit Public High School science teacher who enjoys writing.

He has written numerous Christmas and family based screenplays. Two of his screenplays have won high awards at the Moondance International Film Festival.

Brian is a father of five adult children. He and his wife Cathy live in Canton Michigan .

Snowville is Brian's first book. Watch for Santa's Elf for Christmas 2011.

LaVergne, TN USA
11 December 2010
208340LV00002B

9780982694558